Egy

written by Claire Hawcock
illustrated by Sue Hendra and Paul Linnet

consultant: Bob Rees

A catalogue record for this book is available from the British Library

Published by Ladybird Books Ltd
80 Strand London WC2R 0RL
A Penguin Company

2 4 6 8 10 9 7 5 3 1
© LADYBIRD BOOKS LTD MMVIII
LADYBIRD and the device of a Ladybird are trademarks of Ladybird Books Ltd

Produced by Calcium for Ladybird Books Ltd

ISBN-13: 978 1 84646 924 4

Printed in China

Contents

Some words appear in **bold** in this book.
Turn to the glossary to learn about them.

The ancient Egyptians

The ancient Egyptians lived more than 3,000 years ago along the banks of the River Nile in Egypt. They are well known for their huge buildings, some of which can still be seen today. They also knew a lot about **engineering**, mathematics, medicine and **astronomy**.

the ancient Egyptians built boats, which they sailed along the Nile

many were farmers who worked on the rich flood land next to the Nile

Mediterranean Sea

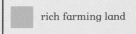
rich farming land

Giza
Saqqara
Lower Egypt

River Nile

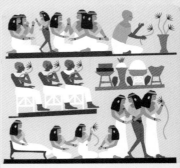

Paintings left behind on
the walls of their buildings
show us how the ancient
Egyptians lived.

Deir el-Bahri
Valley of the Kings • Thebes
Karnak

Red Sea

Upper Egypt

The ancient
Egyptians
mined for gold
between the Nile
and the Red Sea.
Egypt was the
richest country in
Abu Simbel   the ancient world.

7

Pharaohs and queens

Egypt was ruled by pharaohs (*FARE-roes*). Pharaohs were not just kings or queens – they were thought to be gods, too. The pharaoh wore a **nemes**, which looked like a crown of cobras. He also wore a false beard.

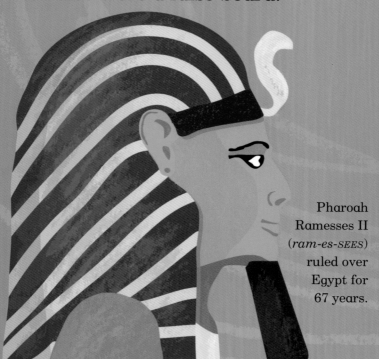

Pharoah Ramesses II (*ram-es-SEES*) ruled over Egypt for 67 years.

Tutankhamun's (*TOOT-an-CAR-moon*) **tomb** was discovered in 1922. It had 5,000 treasures in it, including beautiful jewellery, furniture and sculptures.

Only kings, queens and gods could carry the ankh (*ank*). It was the Egyptian sign of life.

Hatshepsut *(hat-SHEP-sut)* was a powerful woman who ruled Egypt for about twenty years. She wore the pharaoh's crown and beard to show she was as strong as any male king.

9

Gods and goddesses

The Egyptians worshipped many gods and goddesses. They believed that each one looked after them in a different way. Many gods were shown with an animal's head and a human body.

Khnum (*k-NOOM*) had the head of a ram. He looked after the River Nile.

The moon god Thoth had a bird's head. He gave the Egyptians the knowledge of writing, mathematics and medicine.

Amun-Re (*ah-moon-ray*) was the king of the gods. He protected the pharaoh.

The ancient Egyptians built obelisks. These were tall stone monuments. They were decorated with messages to the gods.

Bastet was a cat goddess. She made the sun ripen corn.

11

Making a mummy

The ancient Egyptians believed in life after death. They thought that if they **preserved** the bodies of important people who had died, the dead would pass into the **afterlife**. To preserve bodies, **embalmers** turned them into **mummies**.

1 First, the brain, stomach, liver, lungs and intestines were removed. The body was then covered with salt. That made it dry out.

a priest dressed as Anubis *(an-NOO-bis)*, god of the dead, helped to make the mummy

2 Next, the body was wrapped in two layers of linen bandages.

The body's liver, lungs, stomach and intestines were stored in containers called canopic (*can-OP-ick*) jars.

3 Finally, the mummy was put into a body-shaped coffin. The mummy wore a mask, which was painted to look like the dead person's face.

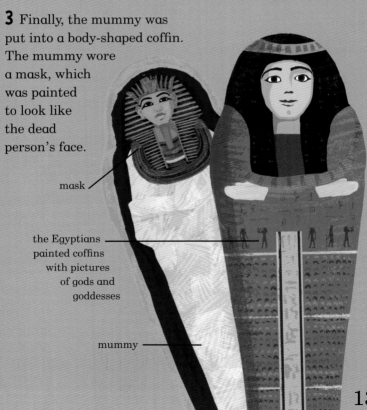

mask

the Egyptians painted coffins with pictures of gods and goddesses

mummy

13

Journey to the afterlife

Before a mummy was buried in its tomb, the Egyptians carried out **ceremonies**. The ceremonies made sure the dead person had a safe journey through the **underworld**.

a priest touched the mummy's mouth with a special stick

a priest dressed as Anubis sometimes held up the mummy during the ceremony

mummy

Opening of the Mouth ceremony

Egyptians believed this ceremony helped the dead person eat, drink and move around in the afterlife. This picture, from an Egyptian wall painting, shows what happened in the ceremony.

Weighing of the Heart Ceremony

The ancient Egyptians believed that a dead person's heart was weighed by Anubis against the 'feather of truth'. If the heart was lighter than the feather it meant the dead person had lived a good life. He could then pass into the underworld, where his body was given to the god Osiris (*os-EYE-ris*).

Osiris ____

the dead

After the ceremonies, the dead person's body was put onto a special boat. It was then sailed down the Nile to its tomb.

Pyramids

Important people, such as pharaohs, were buried in tombs called pyramids. Pyramids had a square base and four sloping, triangular sides. Inside were burial chambers, other rooms, and passageways that led to them.

finished pyramid _____

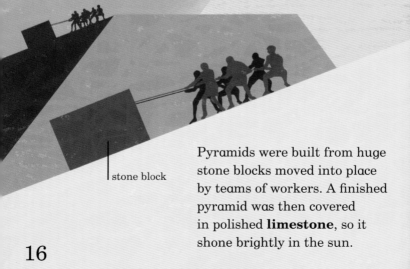

stone block

Pyramids were built from huge stone blocks moved into place by teams of workers. A finished pyramid was then covered in polished **limestone**, so it shone brightly in the sun.

The **burial chamber** was filled with everything a dead person might need in the afterlife. The body was buried with clothes, food and jewellery. Pyramids were sealed after the body was placed inside it.

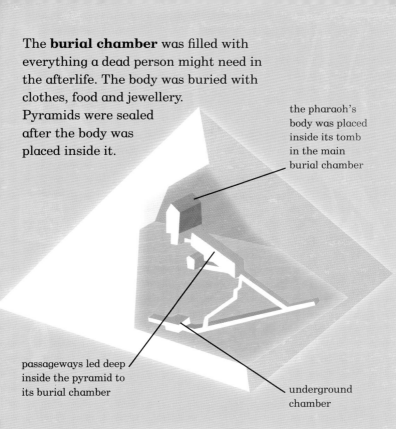

the pharaoh's body was placed inside its tomb in the main burial chamber

passageways led deep inside the pyramid to its burial chamber

underground chamber

Robbers often stole treasure from the Egyptian pyramids.

17

Valley of the Kings

Not all pharaohs were buried in pyramids. Some were buried in underground tombs. The tombs were cut deep into rock in a place called the Valley of the Kings.

In 1922, English **archaeologist** (*ark-ee-OLO-jist*) Howard Carter found the only ancient tomb left untouched by robbers. It belonged to the pharaoh Tutankhamun. It had not been opened for 3,200 years.

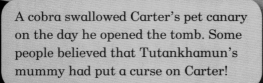

A cobra swallowed Carter's pet canary on the day he opened the tomb. Some people believed that Tutankhamun's mummy had put a curse on Carter!

Inside the burial chamber, Carter found the king's stone coffin, called a **sarcophagus** (*sar-COFF-a-gus*). Within the sarcophagus were three coffins, laid inside each other. The king's mummy was inside the third coffin.

statue of the goddess Bastet

Tutankhamun's sarcophagus

Many beautiful treasures were found inside Tutankhamun's tomb.

If you have a computer, you can download a poster about Tutankhamun from www.ladybird.com/madabout

Temples

Pharaohs and their queens built temples as homes for their gods. The Egyptians visited the temples to worship the gods. They also sometimes used them to celebrate the **reign** of the pharaoh or queen who built them.

The Egyptian queen Hatshepsut is buried near a famous temple at Deir el-Bahri (*DAYR-el-BAR-ee*). The temple would once have had beautiful gardens.

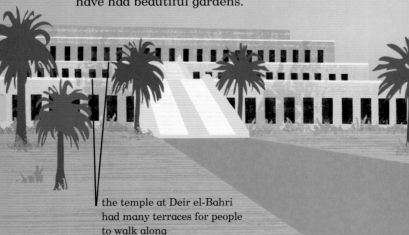

the temple at Deir el-Bahri had many terraces for people to walk along

The temple at Abu Simbel was built by Ramesses II.
Four huge statues of Ramesses decorate the outside.

It took hundreds of years over the reign of thirty
different pharaohs to build the temple at Karnak.

Scribes and writing

Scribes were very important people in ancient Egypt. They started their training at nine years old. Scribes learned how to write hieroglyphs (*hi-RO-glifs*), a form of writing that uses pictures. Hieroglyphs have about 700 different signs.

We have only been able to read hieroglyphs since 1799, when a stone tablet was found at Rosetta in Egypt. Words written in many different languages were found on the Rosetta Stone. Two of the languages were Greek and Egyptian hieroglyphs. The Greek was used to translate the hieroglyphs.

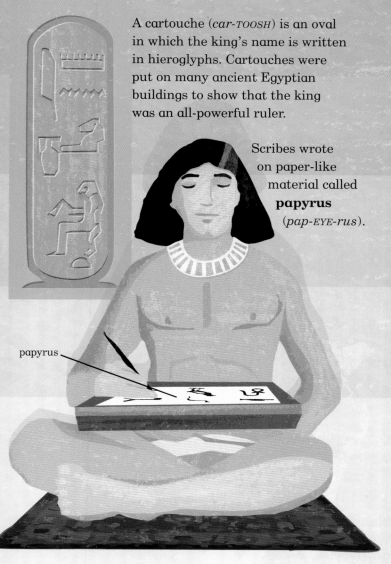

A cartouche (*car-TOOSH*) is an oval in which the king's name is written in hieroglyphs. Cartouches were put on many ancient Egyptian buildings to show that the king was an all-powerful ruler.

Scribes wrote on paper-like material called **papyrus** (*pap-EYE-rus*).

papyrus

23

Toys and games

Egyptian children liked games that are still played today, such as tug-of-war and leapfrog. Skilled craftsmen made children's toys from wood and clay. The ancient Egyptians also invented many board games.

Senet was a board game with two sets of counters that moved along two rows of squares. It is still played today.

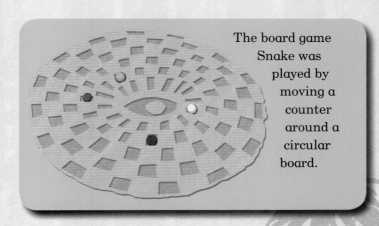

The board game Snake was played by moving a counter around a circular board.

Small children played with clay rattles, wooden horses and wooden dolls.

25

Fantastic facts

- The first pyramid was built at Saqqara. It was a **step pyramid** and was the burial place of King Djoser (*zo-ser*).

- During the pharaoh Akhenaten's (*ACK-en-AY-tun*) reign, the traditional gods and goddesses were **banished**. People were only allowed to worship one god: Aten.

- Six hundred years after the first pyramid was built, all the pyramids had been robbed of their contents.

- The Egyptians buried their dead with hundreds of shabtis. Shabtis were models of servants that worked for the dead in the afterlife.

- Egyptian pharaohs had three different crowns. Lower Egypt had a red crown. Upper Egypt had a white crown. A blue crown was worn in times of war.

- Today, x-rays allow us to look at mummies underneath their bandages. That helps us to learn a lot about the lives of mummies without damaging them.

- The Egyptians **mummified** animals as well as people. They did so because they believed the animals were messengers of the gods.

- The Egyptians loved fashion and beauty. They used **kohl** (*kol*) eyeliner and perfume. They also wore wigs and fine clothes.

- During the mummy-making process, a long hook was used to smash up the brain and pull it out through the dead person's nose.

- The ancient Egyptians didn't use money for a long time. Wages were paid in goods, such as cloth and food.

27

Amazing Egyptian awards

Longest ruler

Pepy II ruled Egypt for about 94 years. He became king when he was just six years old.

Greatest pyramid

The Great Pyramid of Giza was built for King Khufu (*koo-foo*). It took 20 years to build and is 146 metres high. That's about the height of 50 tractors one on top of another!

Largest sculpture

The Great Sphinx at Giza is the largest single stone statue on Earth. It is 20 metres high and 73 metres long – that's the size of a jumbo jet!

Longest papyrus

The Great Harris Papyrus is written in hieroglyphs and has 1,500 lines. It is 41 metres long. That's as long as three and a half buses!

Most beautiful

Queen Nefertari's (*NEFF-er-TAR-ee*) tomb shows pictures of her in life and death. The ceiling is painted dark blue and decorated with gold stars.

Glossary

afterlife – a world in which the Egyptians believed people who had died came to life again.

archaeologist – someone who studies objects from the past to find out more about the people who made them.

astronomy – the study of planets, stars and the universe.

banish – to send away.

burial chamber – the room in which a mummy is left after it has been put in a coffin.

ceremony – an act that is performed at a special time.

embalmer – a person who preserves dead bodies for burial.

engineering – scientific rules used to build or design buildings.

kohl – make-up made from soot and used to darken the eye area.

limestone – a white rock that shines brilliantly in the sun.

mummified – when a body has been embalmed to stop it rotting.

mummy – a body that has been embalmed.

nemes – a crown worn only by the pharaoh.

papyrus – a form of paper made from reeds.

preserve – to stop from rotting.

reign – the time of a king or queen's rule.

sarcophagus – a large stone coffin.

scribe – a person who records things in writing.

step pyramid – a pyramid without smooth sides, showing the steps of stone.

tomb – a building or underground room in which a body is buried.

underworld – a place through which the ancient Egyptians believed a dead person must pass before they could reach the afterlife.